SEVE

RECEIPTS

FOR

PASTRY, CAKES, AND SWEETMEATS.

SEVENTY-FIVE

RECEIPTS,

FOR

PASTRY, CAKES, AND SWEETMEATS.

BY A LADY OF PHILADELPHIA.

APPLEWOOD BOOKS

Applewood Books would like to thank culinary
historian Karen Hess for her generous help in
guiding the historical accuracy of this reprint.

ISBN: 1-55709-116-1

Thank you for purchasing an Applewood Book.
Applewood reprints America's lively classic–books
from the past that are still of interest to modern readers.
For a free copy of our current catalog, please write to:
Applewood Books, Box 365, Bedford, MA 01730.

10 9 8 7 6 5

Library of Congress Cataloging-in-Publication Data
Leslie, Eliza, 1787–1858.
  Seventy-five receipts for pastry, cakes, and sweetmeats /
by a lady of Philadelphia.
    viii, 88 p. ; 19 cm.
    Originally published: Boston: Munroe & Francis, 1828.
    ISBN 1-55709-116-1
    1. Confectionery.   2. Baked products.   3. Cookery
I. Title.
TX765.L63   1993
641.8 – dc20   93-12983
                                                      CIP

A Note to the Reader

Eliza Leslie was a noted author of cookbooks and juveniles during the early part of the nineteenth century. She was the author of one of the most popular nineteenth century cookbooks, *Directions for Cookery*. Mrs. Leslie's reputation, however, was created with this book. When *Seventy-five Receipts for Pastry, Cakes, and Sweetmeats* was published in 1828, it was very favorably received, and a second edition appeared the following year. Because of its popularity, *Seventy-five Receipts...* went through over twenty editions during the nineteenth century in original and expanded forms.

This facsimile is reproduced from the first edition. Early editions of the book were filled with editorial errors. The reader will note that errors which appeared have not been changed.

SEVENTY-FIVE

RECEIPTS,

FOR

PASTRY, CAKES, AND SWEETMEATS.

———◆———

BY A LADY OF PHILADELPHIA.

———◆———

—◦◦◦—

BOSTON:

MUNROE AND FRANCIS, NO. 128, WASHINGTON-STREET,

————————

C. S. FRANCIS, 252 BROADWAY, NEW-YORK.

1828.

PREFACE.

THE following Receipts for Pastry, Cakes, and Sweetmeats, are all original, and have been used by the author and many of her friends with uniform success. They are drawn up in a style so plain and minute, as to be perfectly intelligible to servants, and persons of the most moderate capacity. All the ingredients, with their proper quantities, are enumerated in a list at the head of each receipt, a plan which will greatly facilitate the business of procuring and preparing the requisite articles.

There is frequently much difficulty in following directions in English and French Cookery Books, not only from their want of explicitness, but from the difference in the fuel, fire-places, and cooking utensils generally used in Europe and America; and many of the European receipts are so complicated and laborious, that our female cooks are afraid to undertake the arduous task of making any thing from them.

The receipts in this little book are, in every sense of the word, American ; but the writer flatters herself that (if exactly followed) the articles produced from them will not be found inferior to any of a similar description made in the European manner. Experience has proved, that pastry, cakes, &c. prepared *precisely* according to these directions will not fail to be excellent ; but where economy is expedient, a portion of the seasoning, that is, the spice, wine, brandy, rose-water, essence of lemon, &c. may be omitted without any essential deviation of flavour, or difference of appearance ; retaining, however, the given proportions of eggs, butter, sugar, and flour.

But if done at home, and by a person that can be trusted, it will be proved, on trial, that any of these articles may be made in the best and most liberal manner at *one half* of the cost of the same articles supplied by a confectioner. And they will be found particularly useful to families that live in the country or in small towns, where nothing of the kind is to be purchased.

January 15th, 1828.

CONTENTS.

———

PART THE FIRST.

PART THE SECOND.

PART THE THIRD.

PART THE FIRST.

PASTRY.

———

PRELIMINARY REMARKS.

In making pastry or cakes, it is best to begin by weighing out the ingredients, sifting the flour, pounding and sifting the sugar and spice, washing the butter, and preparing the fruit.

Sugar can be powdered by pounding it in a large mortar, or by rolling it on a paste-board with a rolling-pin. It should be made very fine and always sifted.

All sorts of spice should be pounded in a mortar except nutmeg, which it is better to grate. If spice is wanted in large quantities, it may be ground in a mill.

The butter should always be fresh and very good. Wash it in cold water before you use it, and then make it up with your hands into hard lumps, squeezing the water well out.

If the butter and sugar are to be stirred together, always do that before the eggs are beaten, as, (unless they are kept too warm) the butter and sugar will not be injured by standing awhile. For stirring them, nothing is so convenient as a round hickory stick about a foot and a half long, and somewhat flattened at one end.

The eggs should not be beaten till after all the other ingredients are ready, as they will fall very soon. If the whites and yolks are to be beaten separately, do the whites first, as they will stand longer.

Eggs should be beaten in a broad shallow pan, spreading wide at the top. Butter and sugar should be stirred in a deep pan with straight sides.

Break every egg by itself, in a saucer, before you put it into the pan, that in case there should be any bad ones, they may not spoil the others.

Eggs are beaten most expeditiously with rods. A small quantity of white of egg may be beaten with a knife, or a three-pronged fork.

———

There can be no positive rules as to the exact time of baking each article. Skill in baking is the result of practice, attention, and experience. Much, of course, depends on the state of the fire, and on the size of the things to be baked, and something on the thickness of the pans or dishes.

If you bake in a stove, put some bricks in the oven part to set the pans or plates on, and to temper the heat at the bottom. Large sheets of iron, without sides, will be found very useful for small cakes, and to put under the pans or plates.

PUFF PASTE.

Half a pound and two ounces of sifted flour.
Half a pound of the best fresh butter—washed.
A little cold water.

———

This will make puff-paste for two puddings, or for one soup-plate, or four small shells.

———

Weigh half a pound and two ounces of flour, and sift it through a hair sieve into a large deep dish. Take out about one fourth of the flour, and lay it aside on one corner of your paste-board, to roll and sprinkle with.

Wash, in cold water, half a pound of the best fresh butter. Squeeze it hard with your hands, and make it up into a round lump. Divide it in four equal parts; lay them on one side of your paste-board, and have ready a glass of cold water.

Cut one of the four pieces of butter into the pan of flour. Cut it as small as possible. Wet it, gradually, with a very little water (too much water will make it tough) and mix it well with the point of a large case-knife. Do not touch it with your hands. When the dough gets into a lump, sprinkle on the middle of the board some of the flour that you laid aside, and lay the dough upon it, turning it out of the pan with the knife.

Rub the rolling-pin with flour, and sprinkle a little on the lump of paste. Roll it out thin quickly and evenly, pressing on the rolling-pin very lightly. Then take the second of the four pieces of butter, and, with the point of your knife, stick it in little bits at equal distances all over the sheet of paste. Sprinkle on some flour, and fold up the dough.

Flour the paste-board and rolling-pin again ; throw a little flour on the paste and roll it out a second time. Stick the third piece of butter all over it in little bits. Throw on some flour, fold up the paste, sprinkle a little more flour on the dough, and on the rolling-pin, and roll it out a third time, always pressing on it lightly. Stick it over with the fourth and last piece of butter. Throw on a little more flour, fold up the paste and then roll it out in a large round sheet. Cut off the sides, so as to make the sheet of a square form, and lay the slips of dough upon the square sheet. Fold it up with the small pieces or trimmings, in the inside. Score or notch it a little with the knife ; lay it on a plate and set it away in a cool place, but not where it can freeze, as that will make it heavy. Having made the paste, prepare and mix your pudding or pie. When the mixture is finished, bring out your paste, flour the board and rolling-pin, and roll it out with a short quick stroke, and pressing the rolling-pin rather harder than while you were putting the butter in. If the paste rises in blisters, it will be light, unless spoiled in baking.

Then cut the sheet in half, fold up each piece and roll them out once more, separately, in round sheets the size of your plate. Press on rather harder, but not too hard. Roll the sheets thinnest in the middle and thickest at the edges. If intended for puddings, lay them in buttered soup-plates, and trim them evenly round the edges. If the edges do not appear thick enough, you may take the trimmings, put them all together, roll them out, and having cut them in slips the breadth of the rim of the plate, lay them all round to make the paste thicker at the edges, joining them nicely and evenly, as every patch or crack will appear distinctly when baked. Notch the rim handsomely with a very sharp knife. Fill the dish with the mixture of the pudding, and bake it in a moderate oven. The paste should be of a light brown colour. If the oven is too slow, it will be soft and clammy ; if too quick, it will not have time to rise as high as it ought to do.

In making the best puff-paste, try to avoid using more flour to sprinkle and roll with, than the small portion which you have laid aside for that purpose at the beginning. If you make the dough too soft at first, by using too much water, it will be sticky, and require more flour, and will eventually be tough when baked. Do not put your hands to it, as their warmth will injure it. Use the knife instead. Always roll from you rather than to you, and press lightly on the rolling-pin, except at the last.

It is difficult to make puff-paste in the summer, unless in a cellar, or very cool room, and on a marble table. The butter should, if possible, be washed the night before, and kept covered with ice till you use it next day. The water should have ice in it, and the butter should be iced as it sets on the paste-board. After the paste is mixed, it should be put in a covered dish, and set in cold water till you are ready to give it the last rolling. With all these precautions to prevent its being heavy, it will not rise as well, or be in any respect as good as in cold weather.

COMMON PASTE FOR PIES.

A pound and a half of sifted flour.
Three quarters of a pound of butter—washed.

———

This will make one large pie, or two small ones.

———

Sift the flour into a pan. Put the butter into two equal parts. Put one half of the butter into the flour, and cut it up as small as possible. Mix it well with the flour, wetting it gradually with a little cold water.

Spread some flour on your paste-board, take the lump of paste out of the pan, flour your rolling-pin, and roll out the paste into a large sheet. Then stick it over with the remaining half of the butter in small pieces, and laid at equal distances. Throw on a little flour, fold up the sheet of paste, flour it slightly, and roll it out again. Then fold it up, and cut it in half or in four, according to the size of your pies. Roll it out into round sheets the size of your pie-plates, pressing rather harder on the rolling-pin.

Butter your pie-plates, lay on your under crust, and trim the edge. Fill the dish with the ingredients of which the pie is composed, and lay on the lid, in which you must prick some holes, or cut a small slit in the top. Crimp the edges with a sharp knife.

Heap up the ingredients so that the pie will be highest in the middle.

Some think it makes common paste more crisp and light to beat it hard on both sides with the rolling-pin, after you give it the first rolling, when all the butter is in.

If the butter is very fresh, you may mix with the flour a salt spoonful of salt.

———◆———

MINCE PIES.

One pound and a half of boiled beef's heart, or fresh tongue—chopped when cold.
Two pounds of beef suet, chopped fine.
Four pounds of pippin apples, chopped.
Two pounds of raisins, stoned and chopped.
Two pounds of currants, picked, washed and dried.
Two pounds of powdered sugar.
One quart of white wine.
One quart of brandy.
One wine-glass of rose-water.
Two grated nutmegs.
Half an ounce of cinnamon
A quarter of an ounce of cloves } powdered.
A quarter of an ounce of mace
A tea-spoonful of salt.
Two large oranges.
Half a pound of citron, cut in slips.

————

Parboil a beef's heart, or a fresh tongue. After you have taken off the skin and fat, weigh a pound and a half. When it is cold, chop it very fine. Take the inside of the suet; weigh two pounds, and chop it as fine as possible. Mix the meat and suet together, adding the salt. Pare, core, and chop the apples, and then stone and chop the raisins. Having prepared the currants, add them to the other fruit, and mix the fruit with the meat and suet. Put in the sugar and spice, and the grated peel and juice of the oranges. Wet the whole with the rose-water and liquor, and mix all well together.

2

Make the paste, allowing, for each pie, half a pound of butter and three quarters of a pound of sifted flour. Make it in the same manner as puff-paste, but it will not be quite so rich. Lay a sheet of paste all over a soup-plate. Fill it with mince-meat, laying slips of citron on the top. Roll out a sheet of paste, for the lid of the pie. Put it on, and crimp the edges with a knife. Prick holes in the lid.

Bake the pies half an hour in a brisk oven.

———

Keep your mince-meat in a jar tightly covered. Set it in a dry cool place, and occasionally add more brandy to it.

———

PLUM PUDDING.

One pound of raisins, stoned and cut in half.
One pound of currants, picked, washed, and dried.
One pound of beef suet, chopped fine.
One pound of grated stale bread, or a pound of flour.
Eight eggs.
A quarter of a pound of sugar.
A pint of milk.
A glass of brandy.
A glass of wine.
Two nutmegs, grated.
A table-spoonful of mixed cinnamon and mace.
A salt-spoonful of salt.

———

You must prepare all your ingredients the day before (except beating the eggs) that in the morning you may have nothing to do but to mix them, as the pudding will require six hours to boil.

Beat the eggs very light, then put to them half the milk and beat both together. Stir in gradually the flour or grated bread. Next add the sugar by degrees. Then the suet and fruit alternately. The

fruit must be well sprinkled with flour, lest it sink
to the bottom. Stir very hard. Then add the
spice and liquor, and lastly the remainder of the
milk. Stir the whole mixture very well together.
If it is not thick enough, add a little more grated
bread or flour. If there is too much bread or flour,
the pudding will be hard and heavy.

Dip your pudding-cloth in boiling water, shake it
out and sprinkle it slightly with flour. Lay it in a
pan, and pour the mixture into the cloth. Tie it
up carefully, allowing room for the pudding to
swell. Boil it six hours and turn it carefully out of
the cloth.

Before you send it to table, have ready some
blanched sweet almonds cut in slips, or some slips
of citron, or both. Stick them all over the outside
of the pudding.

Eat it with wine, or with a sauce made of drawn
butter, wine and nutmeg.

The pudding will be improved if you add to the
other ingredients, the grated rind of a large lemon
or orange.

LEMON PUDDING.

One large lemon, with a smooth thin rind.
Three eggs.
A quarter of a pound of powdered white sugar.
A quarter of a pound of fresh butter—washed.
Half a glass of white wine and brandy, mixed.
A tea-spoonful of rose-water.

Five ounces of sifted flour, and a quarter of a pound of fresh butter
for the paste.

Grate the yellow part of the rind of a large fresh
emon. Then cut the lemon in half, and squeeze

the juice into the plate that contains the grated rind, carefully taking out all the seeds. Mix the juice and rind together.

Put a quarter of a pound of powdered white sugar into a deep earthen pan, and cut up in it a quarter of a pound of the best fresh butter. If the weather is very cold, set the pan near the fire, for a few minutes to soften the butter, but do not allow it to melt or it will be heavy. Stir the butter and sugar together with a stick or wooden spoon, till it is perfectly light and of the consistence of cream.

Put the eggs in a shallow broad pan, and beat them with an egg-beater or rods till they are quite smooth, and as thick as a boiled custard. Then stir the eggs, gradually, into the pan of butter and sugar. Add the liquor and rose-water by degrees, and then stir in, gradually, the juice and grated rind of the lemon. Stir the whole very hard, after all the ingredients are in.

Have ready a puff-paste made of five ounces of sifted flour, and a quarter of a pound of fresh butter. The paste must be made with as little water as possible. Roll it out in a circular sheet, thin in the centre, and thicker towards the edges, and just large enough to cover the bottom, sides, and edges of a soup-plate. Butter the soup-plate very well, and lay the paste in it, making it neat and even round the broad edge of the plate. With a sharp knife, trim off the surperfluous dough, and notch the edges. Put in the mixture with a spoon, and bake the pudding about half an hour, in a moderate oven. It should be baked of a very light brown. If the oven is too hot, the paste will not have time to rise well. If too cold, it will be clammy. When the pudding is cool, grate loaf-sugar over it.

ORANGE PUDDING.

One large orange, of a deep colour, and smooth thin rind.
One lime.
A quarter of a pound of powdered white sugar.
A quarter of a pound of fresh butter.
Three eggs.
Half a glass of mixed wine and brandy.
A tea-spoonful of rose-water.

———

Grate the yellow rind of the orange and lime, and squeeze the juice into a saucer or soup-plate, taking out all the seeds.

Stir the butter and sugar to a cream.

Beat the eggs as light as possible, and then stir them by degrees into the pan of butter and sugar. Add, gradually, the liquor and rose-water, and then by degrees, the orange and lime. Stir all well together.

Have ready a sheet of puff-paste made of five ounces of sifted flour, and a quarter of a pound of fresh butter. Lay the paste in a buttered soup-plate. Trim and notch the edges, and then put in the mixture. Bake it about half an hour, in a moderate oven. Grate loaf-sugar over it, before you send it to table.

———◆———

COCOA-NUT PUDDING.

A quarter of a pound of cocoa-nut, grated.
A quarter of a pound of powdered white sugar.
Three ounces and a half of fresh butter.
The whites only of six eggs.
Half a glass of wine and brandy mixed.
Half a tea-spoonful of rose-water.

———

Break up a cocoa-nut, and take the thin brown skin carefully off, with a knife. Wash all the

2*

pieces in cold water, and then wipe them dry, with a clean towel. Weigh a quarter of a pound of cocoa-nut, and grate it very fine, into a soup-plate.

Stir the butter and sugar to a cream, and add the liquor and rose-water gradually to them.

Beat the whites only of six eggs, till they stand alone on the rods ; and then stir the beaten white of egg gradually into the butter and sugar. Afterwards sprinkle in, by degrees, the grated cocoanut, stirring hard all the time. Then stir all very well at the last.

Have ready a puff-paste sufficient to cover the bottom, sides, and edges of a soup-plate. Put in the mixture, and bake it in a moderate oven, about half an hour.

Grate loaf-sugar over it, when cool.

ALMOND PUDDING.

Half a pound of sweet almonds, which will be reduced to a quarter of a pound when shelled and blanched.
An ounce of blanched bitter almonds or peach-kernels.
The whites only of six eggs.
A quarter of a pound of butter.
A quarter of a pound of powdered white sugar.
Half a glass of mixed brandy, wine, and rose-water.

Shell half a pound of sweet almonds, and pour scalding water over them, which will make the skins peal off. As they get cool, pour more boiling water, till the almonds are all blanched. Blanch also the bitter almonds. As you blanch the almonds, throw them into a bowl of cold water. Then take them out, one by one, wipe them dry in a clean towel, and lay them on a plate. Pound them one at a time to a fine paste, in a marble mortar, adding, as you pound them, a few drops of rose-water to prevent their oiling. Pound the bitter and sweet almonds alternately, that they may be well mixed. They must be made perfectly fine and smooth, and are the better for being prepared the day before they are wanted for the pudding.

Stir the butter and sugar to a cream, and add to it, gradually, the liquor.

Beat the whites of six eggs till they stand alone. Stir the almonds and white of eggs, alternately, into the butter and sugar; and then stir the whole well together.

Have ready a puff-paste sufficient for a soup-plate. Butter the plate, lay on the paste, trim and notch it. Then put in the mixture.

Bake it about half an hour in a moderate oven.

Grate loaf-sugar over it.

A CHEESECAKE.

Four eggs.
Half a gill of milk.
A quarter of a pound of butter.
A quarter of a pound of powdered sugar.
Two ounces of grated bread.
Half a glass of mixed brandy and wine.
A tea-spoonful of rose-water.
A tea-spoonful of mace, cinnamon, and nutmeg, mixed.
A quarter of a pound of currants.

Pick the currants very clean. Wash them through a cullender, wipe them in a towel, and then dry them on a dish before the fire.

When dry, take out a few to scatter over the

top of the cheesecake, lay them aside, and sprinkle
the remainder of the currants with flour.

Stir the butter and sugar to a cream.   Grate the
bread, and prepare the spice.   Beat the eggs very
light.

Boil the milk.   When it comes to a boil, add to
it half the beaten egg, and boil both together till it
becomes a curd, stirring it frequently with a knife.
Then throw the grated bread on the curd, and stir
all together.   Then take the milk, egg, and bread
off the fire, and stir it, gradually, into the butter
and sugar.   Next, stir in the remaining half of
the egg.

Add, by degrees, the liquor and spice.

Lastly, stir in, gradually, the currants.

Have ready a puff-paste, which should be made
before you prepare the cheesecake, as the mixture
will become heavy by standing.   Before you put it
into the oven, scatter the remainder of the currants
over the top.

Bake it half an hour in rather a quick oven.

Do not sugar the top.

You may bake it either in a soup-plate, or in two
small tin patty-pans, which, for cheesecakes, should
be of a square shape.   If baked in square patty-
pans, leave at each side a flap of paste in the shape
of a half-circle.   Put long slits in these flaps, and
turn them over, so that they will rest on the top
of the mixture.

You can, if you chuse, add to the currants a few
raisins stoned, and cut in half.

SWEET POTATO PUDDING.

A quarter of a pound of boiled sweet potato.
Three eggs.
A quarter of a pound of powdered white sugar.
A quarter of a pound of fresh butter.
A glass of mixed wine and brandy.
A half-glass of rose-water.
A tea-spoonful of mixed spice, nutmeg, mace and cinnamon.

———

Pound the spice, allowing a smaller proportion of mace than of nutmeg and cinnamon.

Boil and peal some sweet potatoes, and when they are cold, weigh a quarter of a pound. Mash the sweet potato very smooth, and rub it through a sieve. Stir the sugar and butter to a cream.

Beat the eggs very light, and stir them into the butter and sugar, alternately with the sweet potato. Add by degrees the liquor, rose-water and spice. Stir all very hard together.

Spread puff-paste on a soup-plate. Put in the mixture, and bake it about half an hour in a moderate oven.

Grate sugar over it.

———

PUMPKIN PUDDING.

A quarter of a pound of stewed pumpkin.
Three eggs.
A quarter of a pound of fresh butter, or a pint of cream.
A quarter of a pound of powdered white sugar.
Half a glass of wine and brandy mixed.
Half a glass of rose-water.
A tea-spoonful of mixed spice, nutmeg, mace and cinnamon.

———

Stew some pumpkin with as little water as possible. Drain it in a cullender, and press it till dry. When cold, weigh a quarter of a pound, and pass it through a sieve. Prepare the spice. Stir together the sugar, and butter, or cream, till they are perfectly light. Add to them, gradually, the spice and liquor.

Beat three eggs very light, and stir them into the butter and sugar alternately with the pumpkin.

Cover a soup-plate with puff-paste, and put in the mixture. Bake it in a moderate oven about half an hour.

Grate sugar over it, when cool.

Instead of the butter, you may boil a pint of milk or cream, and when cold, stir into it in turn the sugar, eggs, and pumpkin.

GOOSEBERRY PUDDING.

A pint of stewed gooseberries, with all their juice.
A quarter of a pound of powdered sugar.
Two ounces of fresh butter.
Two ounces of grated bread.
Three eggs.

Stew the gooseberries till quite soft. When they are cold, mash them fine with the back of a spoon, and stir into them two ounces of sugar. Take two ounces more of sugar, and stir it to a cream with two ounces of butter.

Grate very fine, as much stale bread as will weigh two ounces.

Beat three eggs, and stir them into the butter and sugar, in turn with the gooseberries, and bread.

Lay puff-paste in a soup-plate. Put in the mixture, and bake it half an hour.

Do not grate sugar over it.

BAKED APPLE PUDDING.

A pint of stewed apple.
Half a pint of cream, or two ounces of butter.
A quarter of a pound of powdered sugar.
A nutmeg, grated.
A table-spoonful of rose water.
A tea-spoonful of grated lemon-peel.

Stew your apple in as little water as possible, and not long enough for the pieces to break and lose their shape. Put them in a cullender to drain, and mash them with the back of a spoon. If stewed too long, and in too much water, they will lose their flavour. When cold, mix with them the nutmeg, rose-water, and lemon-peel, and two ounces of sugar. Stir the other two ounces of sugar, with the butter or cream, and then mix it gradually with the apple.

Bake it in puff-paste, in a soup-dish about half an hour in a moderate oven.

Do not sugar the top.

FRUIT PIES.

Fruit pies for family use, are generally made with common paste, allowing three quarters of a pound of butter to a pound and a half of flour.

Peaches and plums, for pies, should be cut in half, and the stones taken out. Cherries also should be stoned, and red cherries only should be used for pies.

Apples should be cut into very thin slices, and are much improved by a little lemon-peel. Sweet apples are not good for pies, as they are very insipid when baked, and seldom get thoroughly done. If green apples are used, they should first be stewed in as little water as possible, and made very sweet.

Apples, stewed previous to baking, should not be done till they break, but only till they are tender. They should then be drained in a cullender, and chopped fine with a knife or the edge of a spoon.

In making pies of juicy fruit, it is a good way to set a small tea-cup on the bottom crust, and lay the fruit all round it. The juice will collect under the cup, and not run out at the edges or top of the pie. The fruit should be mixed with a sufficient quantity of sugar, and piled up in the middle, so as to make the pie highest in the centre. The upper crust should be pricked with a fork, or have a slit cut in the middle. The edges should be nicely crimped with a knife.

Dried peaches, dried apples, and cranberries should be stewed with a very little water, and allowed to get quite cold before they are put into the pie. If stewed fruit is put in warm, it will make the paste heavy.

If your pies are made in the form of shells, or without lids, the fruit should always be stewed first, or it will not be sufficiently done, as the shells (which should be of puff-paste) must not bake so long as covered pies.

Shells intended for sweetmeats, must be baked empty, and the fruit put into them before they go to table.

Fruit pies with lids, should have loaf-sugar grated over them. If they have been baked the day before, they should be warmed in the stove, or near the fire, before they are sent to table, to soften the crust, and make them taste fresh.

Raspberry and apple-pies are much improved by taking off the lid, and pouring in a little cream, just before they go to table. Replace the lid very carefully.

* * *

OYSTER PIE.

A hundred large fresh oysters, or more if small.
The yolks of six eggs boiled hard.
A large slice of stale-bread, grated.
A tea-spoonful of salt.
A table-spoonful of pepper.
A table-spoonful of mixed spice, nutmeg, mace and cinnamon.

———

Take a large round dish, butter it, and spread a rich paste over the sides, and round the edge, but not at the bottom.

Salt oysters will not do for pies. They should be fresh, and as large and fine as possible.

Drain off part of the liquor from the oysters. Put them into a pan, and season them with pepper, salt and spice. Stir them well with the seasoning. Have ready the yolks of eggs, chopped fine, and the grated bread. Pour the oysters (with as much of their liquor as you please) into the dish that has the paste in it. Strew over them the chopped egg and grated bread.

Roll out the lid of the pie, and put it on, crimping the edges handsomely.

Take a small sheet of paste, cut it into a square

3

and roll it up.   Cut it with a sharp knife into the
form of a double tulip.

Make a slit in the centre of the upper crust, and
stick the tulip in it.

Cut out eight large leaves of paste, and lay them
on the lid.

Bake the pie in a quick oven.

––––

If you think the oysters will be too much done
by baking them in the crust, you can substitute
for them, pieces of bread, to keep up the lid of
the pie.

Put the oysters with their liquor and the seasoning, chopped egg, grated bread, &c. into a pan.
Cover them closely, and let them just come to a
boil, taking them off the fire, and stirring them frequently.

When the crust is baked, take the lid neatly off
(loosening it round the edge with a knife) take out
the pieces of bread, and put in the oysters. Lay
the lid on again very carefully.

––––

For oyster patties, the oysters are prepared in the
same manner. They may be chopped if you choose.
They must be put in small shells of puff-paste.

––◆––

BEEF-STEAK PIE.

Butter a deep dish, and spread a sheet of paste
all over the bottom, sides, and edge.

Cut away from your beef-steak all the bone, fat,
gristle, and skin. Cut the lean in small thin pieces,
about as large, generally, as the palm of your hand.
Beat the meat well with the rolling-pin, to make it

juicy and tender. If you put in the fat, it will make the gravy too greasy and strong, as it cannot be skimmed.

Put a layer of meat over the bottom-crust of your dish, and season it to your taste, with pepper, salt, and, if you choose, a little nutmeg. A small quantity of mushroom ketchup is an improvement ; so also, is a little minced onion.

Have ready some cold boiled potatoes sliced thin. Spread over the meat, a layer of potatoes, and a small piece of butter; then another layer of meat, seasoned, and then a layer of potatoes, and so on till the dish is full and heaped up in the middle, having a layer of meat on the top. Pour in a little water.

Cover the pie with a sheet of paste, and trim the edges. Notch it handsomely with a knife ; and, if you choose, make a tulip of paste, and stick it in the middle of the lid, and lay leaves of paste round it.

———

Fresh oysters will greatly improve a beef-steak pie. So also will mushrooms.

Any meat pie may be made in a similar manner.

———◆———

INDIAN PUDDING.

A pound of beef-suet, chopped very fine.
A pint of molasses.
A pint of rich milk.
Four eggs.
A large tea-spoonful of powdered nutmeg **and cinnamon.**
A little grated or chipped lemon-peel.
Indian meal sufficient to make a thick batter.

———

Warm the milk and molasses, and stir them together. Beat the eggs, and stir them gradually into the milk and molasses, in turn with the suet

and indian meal.   Add the spice and lemon-peel,
and stir all very hard together.   Take care not to
put too much indian meal, or the pudding will be
heavy and solid,

Dip the cloth in boiling water.   Shake it out,
and flour it slightly.   Pour the mixture into it, and
tie it up, leaving room for the pudding to swell.
Boil it three hours.   Serve it up hot, and eat
it with sauce made of drawn butter, wine and
nutmeg.

When cold, it is very good cut in slices and fried.

BATTER PUDDING.

Six eggs.
Eight table-spoonfuls of sifted flour.
One quart of milk.
A salt-spoonful of salt.

Stir the flour, gradually, into the milk, carefully
dissolving all the lumps.   Beat the eggs very light,
and add them by degrees to the milk and flour.
Put in the salt, and stir the whole well together.

Take a very thick pudding-cloth.   Dip it in
boiling water and flour it.   Pour into it the mixture
and tie it up, leaving room for it to swell.   Boil it
hard, one hour, and keep it in the pot, till it is
time to send it to table.   Serve it up with wine-
sauce.

A square cloth, which when tied up will make the
pudding of a round form, is better than a bag.

Apple Batter Pudding is made by pouring the
batter over a dish of pippins, pared, cored, and
sweetened, either whole or cut in pieces.   Bake it,
and eat it with butter and sugar.

BREAD PUDDING.

A quarter of a pound of grated stale bread.
A quart of milk, boiled with two or three sticks of cinnamon, slight-
ly broken.
Eight eggs.
A quarter of a pound of sugar.
A little grated lemon-peel.

———

Boil the milk with the cinnamon, strain it, and
set it away till quite cold.

Grate as much crumb of stale-bread as will weigh
a quarter of a pound. Beat the eggs, and when
the milk is cold, stir them into it, in turn with the
bread and sugar. Add the lemon-peel, and if you
choose, a table-spoonful of rose-water.

Bake it in a buttered dish, and grate nutmeg
over it when done. Do not send it to table hot.
Baked puddings should never be eaten till they
have become cold, or at least cool.

———

RICE PUDDING.

A quarter of a pound of rice.
A quarter of a pound of butter.
A quarter of a pound of sugar.
A pint and a half of milk, or cream and milk.
Six eggs.
A tea-spoonful of mixed spice, mace, nutmeg and cinnamon.
A half wine-glass of rose-water.

———

Wash the rice. Boil it till very soft. Drain it,
and set it away to get cold. Put the butter and
sugar together in a pan, and stir them till very
light. Add to them the spice and rose-water.
Beat the eggs very light, and stir them, gradually,
3*

into the milk. Then stir the eggs and milk into the
butter and sugar, alternately with the rice.

Bake it and grate nutmeg over the top.

Currants or raisins, floured, and stirred in at the
last, will greatly improve it.

It should be eaten cold, or quite cool.

BOSTON PUDDING.

Make a good common paste with a pound and a
half of flour, and three quarters of a pound of butter. When you roll it out the last time, cut off
the edges, till you get the sheet of paste of an even
square shape.

Have ready some fruit sweetened to your taste.
If cranberries, gooseberries, dried peaches, or dam-
sons, they should be stewed, and made very sweet.
If apples, they should be stewed in a very little water, drained, and seasoned with nutmeg, rose-water
and lemon. If currants, raspberries, or blackber-
ries, they should be mashed with sugar, and put
into the pudding raw.

Spread the fruit very thick, all over the sheet of
paste, (which must not be rolled out too thin.)
When it is covered all over with the fruit, roll it
up, and close the dough at both ends, and down
the last side. Tie the pudding in a cloth and
boil it.

Eat it with sugar. It must not be taken out of
the pot till just before it is brought to table.

FRITTERS.

Seven eggs.
Half a pint of milk.
A salt-spoonful of salt.
Sufficient flour to make a thick batter.

Beat the eggs well and stir them gradually into the milk. Add the salt, and stir in flour enough to make a thick batter.

Fry them in lard, and serve them up hot.

Eat them with wine and sugar.

They are improved by stirring in a table-spoonful of yeast.

They are excellent with the addition of cold stewed apple, stirred into the mixture, in which case use less flour.

FINE CUSTARDS.

A quart of milk or cream.
The yolks only, of sixteen eggs.
Six ounces of powdered white sugar.
Half an ounce of cinnamon, broken in small pieces.
A large handful of peach-leaves, or half an ounce of peach-kernels
or bitter almonds, broken in pieces.
A table-spoonful of rose-water.
A nutmeg.

Boil in the milk the cinnamon, and the peach-leaves, or peach-kernels. When it has boiled, set it away to get cold. As soon as it is cold, strain it through a sieve, to clear it from the cinnamon, peach-leaves, &c. and stir into it, gradually, the sugar, spice, and rose-water.

Beat the yolks of sixteen eggs very light, and

stir them by degrees into the milk, which must be quite cold or the eggs will make it curdle. Put the custard into cups and set them in a baking pan, half filled with water. When baked, grate some nutmeg over each, and ice them. Make the icing of the whites of eight eggs, a large tea-spoonful of powdered loaf-sugar, and six drops of essence of lemon, beaten all together till it stands alone. Pile up some of the icing on the top of each custard, heaping it high. Put a spot of red nonpareils on the middle of the pile of icings.

———

If the weather is damp, or the eggs not new-laid, more than eight whites will be required for the icing.

———

PLAIN CUSTARDS.

A quart of rich milk.
Eight eggs.
A quarter of a pound of powdered sugar.
A handful of peach-leaves, or half an ounce of peach-kernels, broken in pieces.
A nutmeg.

———

Boil the peach-leaves or kernels in the milk, and set it away to cool. When cold, strain out the leaves or kernels, and stir in the sugar. Beat the eggs very light, and stir them gradually into the milk, when it is quite cold. Bake it in cups, or in a large white dish.

When cool, grate nutmeg over the top.

RICE CUSTARDS.

Half a pound of rice.
Half a pound of raisins or currants.
Eight yolks of eggs, or six whole eggs.
Six ounces of powdered sugar.
A quart of rich milk.
A handful of peach-leaves, or half an ounce of peach-kernels, broken in pieces.
Half an ounce of cinnamon, broken in pieces,

———

Boil the rice with the raisins or currants, which must first be floured. Butter some cups or a mould, and when the rice is quite soft, drain it, and put it into them. Set it away to get cold.

Beat the eggs well. Boil the milk with the cinnamon, and peach-leaves, or kernels. As soon as it has come to a boil, take it off and strain it through a sieve. Then set it again on the fire, stir into it alternately, the egg and sugar, taking it off frequently, and stirring it hard, lest it become a curd. Take care not to boil it too long, or it will be lumpy, and lose its flavour. When done, set it away to cool. Turn out the rice from the cups or mould, into a deep dish. Pour some of the boiled custard over it, and send up the remainder of the custard in a sauce-boat.

You may, if you choose, ornament the lumps of rice, (after the custard is poured round them) by making a stiff froth of white of egg (beaten till it stands alone) and a few drops of essence of lemon, with a very little powdered loaf-sugar. Heap the froth on the top of each lump of rice.

COLD CUSTARDS.

A quart of new milk, and half a pint of cream, mixed.
A quarter of a pound of powdered white sugar.
A large glass of white wine.
A nutmeg.

———

Mix together the milk, cream, and sugar. Stir
the wine into it, and pour the mixture into your
custard-cups. Set them in a warm place near the
fire, till they become a firm curd. Then set them
on ice, or in a very cold place. Grate nutmeg
over them.

———

CURDS AND WHEY.

Take a small piece of rennet about two inches
square. Wash it very clean in cold water to
get all the salt off, and wipe it dry. Put it in a
tea-cup and pour on it just enough of lukewarm
water to cover it. Let it set all night or for several hours. Then take out the rennet, and stir the
water in which it was soaked, into a quart of milk,
which should be in a broad dish.

Set the milk in a warm place, till it becomes a
firm curd. As soon as the curd is completely
made, set it in a cool place, or on ice (if in summer) for two or three hours before you want to
use it.

Eat it with wine, sugar, and nutmeg.

———

The whey, drained from the curd, is an excellent drink for invalids.

A TRIFLE.

A quart of cream.
A quarter of a pound of loaf-sugar, powdered.
Half a pint of white wine ⎫ mixed.
Half a gill of brandy ⎭
Eight maccaroons, or more if you choose.
Four small spunge-cakes or Naples Biscuit.
Two ounces of blanched sweet almonds, pounded in a mortar.
One ounce of blanched bitter almonds or peach-kernels.
The juice and grated peel of two lemons.
A nutmeg, grated.
A glass of noyau.
A pint of rich boiled custard, made of the yolks of eggs.

Pound the sweet and bitter almonds to a smooth paste, adding a little rose-water as you pound them.

Grate the yellow peel of the lemons, and squeeze the juice into a saucer.

Break the spunge-cake and maccaroons into small pieces, mix them with the almonds, and lay them in the bottom of a large glass bowl. Grate a nutmeg over them, and the juice and peel of the lemons. Add the wine and brandy, and let the mixture remain untouched, till the cakes are dissolved in the liquor. Then stir it a little.

Boil a pint of milk with a few peach-leaves. Strain it, and set it again on the fire. Beat the yolks of six eggs, and stir them into the milk, alternately with four ounces of powdered white sugar. While the custard is boiling, take it frequently off the fire, and stir to prevent its curdling. When done, set it away to cool.

Mix the cream and sugar with a glass of noyau, and beat it with a whisk or rods, till it stands alone.

As the froth rises, take it off with a spoon, and lay it on a sieve (with a large dish under it) to drain. The cream, that drains into the dish, must be poured back into the pan with the rest and beaten over again.   When the cream is finished, set it in a cool place.

When the boiled custard is cold, pour it into the glass bowl upon the dissolved cakes, &c. and when the cream is ready, fill up the bowl with it, heaping it high in the middle.   You may ornament it with nonpareils.

If you choose, you can put in, between the custard and the frothed cream, a layer of fruit jelly, or small fruit preserved.

WHIPT CREAM.

A quart of cream.
The whites of four eggs.
Half a pint of white wine.
A quarter of a pound of powdered loaf-sugar.
Ten drops of strong essence of lemon, or two lemons cut in thin
  slices, or the juice of a large lemon.

Mix together, in a broad pan, all the ingredients, unless you use slices of lemon, and then they must be laid at intervals among the froth, as you heap it in the bowl.

With a whisk or rods, beat the cream to a strong froth.   Have beside your pan a sieve (bottom upwards) with a large dish under it.   As the froth rises, take it lightly off with a spoon, and lay it on the sieve to drain.   When the top of the sieve is full, transfer the froth to a large glass or china bowl.   Continue to do this till the bowl is full.

The cream which has dropped through the sieve into the dish, must be poured into the pan, and beaten over again.   When all the cream is converted into froth, pile it up in the bowl, making it highest in the middle.

If you choose, you may ornament it with red and green nonpareils.

————

If you put in glasses, lay a little jelly in the bottom of each glass, and pile the cream on it.

Keep it in a cool place till you want to use it.

———◆———

FLOATING ISLAND.

Six whites of eggs.
Six large table-spoonfuls of jelly.
A pint of cream.

————

Put the jelly and white of egg into a pan, and beat it together with a whisk, till it becomes a stiff froth, and stands alone.

Have ready the cream, in a broad shallow dish. Just before you send it to table, pile up the froth in the centre of the cream.

———◆———

ICE CREAM.

A quart of rich cream.
Half a pound of powdered loaf-sugar.
The juice of two large lemons, or a pint of strawberries or raspberries.

————

Put the cream into a broad pan, and squeeze the lemon juice into it, or stir in gradually the strawberries or raspberries, which must first be mashed to a smooth paste. Then stir in the sugar by degrees, and when all is well mixed, strain it through a sieve.

Put it into a tin that has a close cover, and set it
4

in a tub.   Fill the tub with ice broken into very
small pieces, and strew among the ice a large quantity of salt,taking care that none of the salt gets into
the cream.   Scrape the cream down with a spoon
as it freezes round the edges of the tin.   When it
is all frozen, dip the tin in lukewarm water ; take out
the cream, and fill your glasses ; but not till a few
minutes before you want to use it, as it will very
soon melt.

You may heighten the colour of the red fruit, by
a little cochineal.

If you wish to have it in moulds, put the cream
into them as soon as it has frozen in the tin.   Set
the moulds in a tub of ice and salt.   Just before
you want to use the cream, take the moulds out of
the tub, wipe or wash the salt, carefully from the
outside, dip the moulds in lukewarm water, and
turn out the cream.

◆

CALVES-FEET JELLY.

Four calves feet.
Three quarts of water.
A pint of white wine.
Three lemons.
The whites of six eggs.
Half an ounce of cinnamon.
Half a pound of loaf-sugar, broken into lumps.

Endeavour to procure calves feet, that have been
nicely singed, but not skinned, as the skin being
left on, makes the jelly much firmer.

The day before you want to use the jelly, boil
the four calves feet in three quarts of water, till
the meat drops from the bone.   When sufficiently

done, put it into a cullender or sieve, and let the
liquid drain from the meat, into a broad pan cr dish.
Skim off the fat. Let the jelly stand till next day,
and then carefully scrape off the sediment from
the bottom. It will be a firm jelly, if too much
water has not been used, and if it has boiled long
enough.

Early next morning, put the jelly into a tin kettle, or covered tin pan ; set it on the fire, and melt
it a little. Take it off, and season it with the cinnamon slightly broken, a pint of madeira wine, three
lemons cut in thin slices, and half a pound of loaf-
sugar, broken up.

If you wish it high-coloured, add two table-spoonfuls of French brandy. Mix all well together.
Beat, slightly, the whites of six eggs (sav.ng the
egg-shells) and stir the whites into the jelly. Break
up the egg-shells into very small pieces, and throw
them in also. Stir the whole very well together.

Set it on the fire, and boil it hard five minutes,
but do not stir it, as that will prevent its clear-
ing. Have ready a large white flannel bag, the
top wide, and the bottom tapering to a point.
Tie the bag to the backs of two chairs, or to the
legs of a table, and set a white dish or a nould
under it.

After the jelly has boiled five minutes, pour it
hot into the bag, and let it drip through into the
dish. Do not squeeze the bag, as that will make
the jelly dull and cloudy.

If it is not clear the first time it passes through
the bag, empty out all the ingredients, wash the
bag, suspend it again, put another white dish under
it, pour the jelly back into the bag, and let it drip
through again. Repeat this six or eight times, or
till it is clear, putting a clean dish under it every

time. If it does not drip freely, move the bag into a warmer place.

When the jelly has all dripped through the bag, and is clear, set it in a cool place to congeal. It will sometimes congeal immediately, and sometimes not for several hours; particularly if the weather is warm and damp. If the weather is very cold, you must take care not to let it freeze. When it is quite firm, which perhaps it will not be till evening, fill your glasses with it, piling it up very high. If you make it in a mould, you must either set the mould under the bag while it is dripping, or pour it from the dish into the mould while it is liquid. When it is perfectly congealed, dip the mould for an instant in boiling water to loosen the jelly. Turn it out on a glass dish.

This quantity of ingredients will make a quart of jelly when finished. In cool weather, it may be made a day or two before it is wanted.

You may increase the seasoning, (that is, the wine, lemon, and cinnamon,) according to your taste, but less than the above proportion will not be sufficient to flavour the jelly.

———

BLANCMANGE.

Four calves feet.
A pint and a half of thick cream.
Half a pound of loaf-sugar, broken up.
A glass of wine.
Half a glass of rose-water.
A tea-spoonful of mace, beaten and sifted.

———

Get four calves feet ; if possible some that have been singed, and not skinned. Scrape, and clean them well, and boil them in three quarts of water, till all the meat drops off the bone. Drain the liquid through a cullender or sieve, and skim it well. Let it stand till next morning, to congeal. Then clean it well from the sediment, and put it into a tin or bell-metal kettle. Stir into it, the cream, sugar, and mace. Boil it hard for five minutes, stirring it several times. Then strain it through a linen cloth or napkin into a large bowl, and add the wine and rose-water.

Set it in a cool place for three or four hours, stirring it very frequently with a spoon to prevent the cream from separating from the jelly. The more it is stirred the better. Stir it till it is cool.

Wash your moulds, wipe them dry, and then wet them with cold water. When the blancmange becomes very thick, (that is, in three or four hours, if the weather is not too damp) put it into your moulds.

When it has set in them till it is quite firm, loosen it carefully all round with a knife, and turn it out on glass or china plates.

––––––––

If you wish to make it with almonds, take an ounce of blanched bitter almonds, and two ounces of sweet. Beat them in a mortar to a fine paste, pouring in occasionally a little rose-water. When the mixture is ready to boil, add the almonds to it, gradually, stirring them well in. Or you may stir them in, while it is cooling in the bowl.

If it inclines to stick to the moulds, set them an instant in hot water. It will then turn out easily.

––––––––

If you choose to make it without calves feet, you can substitute an ounce of the best and clearest isinglass, (or, if in summer, an ounce and a quarter) boiled with the other ingredients. If made with

4*

isinglass, you must use two ounces of sweet, and an
ounce of bitter almonds, with the addition of the
grated rind of a large lemon, and a large stick of
cinnamon, broken up, a glass of wine and half a
glass of rose-water. These ingredients must be all
mixed together, with a quart of cream, and boiled
hard for five minutes. The mixture must then be
strained through a napkin, into a large bowl. Set
it in a cool place, and stir it frequently till nearly
cold. It must then be put into the moulds.

You may substitute for the almonds, half a gill of
noyau, in which case, omit the wine.

PART THE SECOND.

CAKES.

GENERAL DIRECTIONS.

In making cakes, it is particularly necessary that the eggs should be well beaten. They are not sufficiently light, till the surface looks smooth and level, and till they get so thick as to be of the consistence of boiled custard.

White of egg should always be beaten till it becomes a heap of stiff froth, without any liquid at the bottom ; and till it hangs from the rods or fork without dropping.

Eggs become light soonest when new-laid, and when beaten near the fire, or in warm dry weather.

Butter and sugar should be stirred till it looks like thick cream, and till it stands up in the pan.

It should be kept cool. If too warm, it will make the cakes heavy.

Large cakes should be baked in tin or earthen pans, with straight sides, that are as nearly perpendicular as possible. They cut into handsomer slices, and if they are to be iced, it will be found very inconvenient to put on the icing, if the cake slopes in much towards the bottom.

Before you ice a cake, dredge it all over with

flour, and then wipe the flour off. This will enable you to spread on the icing more evenly.

Before you cut an ice cake, cut the icing by it-self with a small sharp penknife. The large knife with which you divide the cake, will crack and break the icing.

Large Gingerbread, as it burns very easily, may be baked in an earthen pan. So also may Black Cake or Pound Cake. Earthen pans or moulds, with a hollow tube in the middle, are best for cakes.

If large cakes are baked in tin pans, the bottom and sides should be covered with sheets of paper, before the mixture is put in. The paper must be well buttered.

Spunge cakes, and Almond cakes should be baked in pans that are as thin as possible.

If the cakes should get burnt, scrape them with a knife or grater, as soon as they are cool.

Always be careful to butter your pans well. Should the cakes stick, they cannot be got out without breaking.

For queen-cakes, &c. the small tins of a round or oval shape are most convenient. Fill them but little more than half.

After the mixture is completed, set it in a cool place till all the cakes are baked.

In rolling out cakes made of dough, use as little flour as possible. When you lay them in the pans, do not place them too close together, lest they run into each other.

When you are cutting them out, dip the cutter frequently in flour, to prevent its sticking.

QUEEN CAKE.

One pound of powdered white sugar.
One pound of fresh butter—washed.
Fourteen ounces of sifted flour.
Ten eggs.
One wine-glass of wine and brandy, mixed.
Half a glass of rose-water, or twelve drops of essence of lemon.
One tea-spoonful of mace and cinnamon, mixed.
One nutmeg, beaten or grated.

Pound the spice to a fine powder, in a marble mortar, and sift it well.

Put the sugar into a deep earthen pan, and cut the butter into it. Stir them together, till very light.

Beat the eggs in a broad shallow pan, till they are perfectly smooth and thick.

Stir into the butter and sugar a little of the beaten egg, and then a little flour, and so on alternately, a little egg and a little flour, till the whole is in ; continuing all the time to beat the eggs, and stirring the mixture very hard. Add by degrees, the spice, and then the liquor, a little at a time. Finally, put in the rose-water, or essence of lemon. Stir the whole very hard at the last.

Take about two dozen little tins, or more, if you have room for them in the oven. Rub them very well with fresh butter. With a spoon, put some of the mixture in each tin, but do not fill them to the top, as the cakes will rise high in baking. Bake them in a quick oven, about a quarter of an hour. When they are done, they will shrink a little from the sides of the tins.

Before you fill the tins again, scrape them well with a knife, and wash or wipe them clean.

If the cakes are scorched by too hot a fire, do

not scrape off the burnt parts, till they have
grown cold.

Make an icing with the whites of three eggs,
beaten till it stands alone, and twenty-four tea-
spoonfuls of the best loaf-sugar, powdered, and
beaten gradually into the white of egg. Flavour it
with a tea-spoonful of rose-water or eight drops of
essence of lemon, stirred in at the last. Spread
it evenly with a broad knife, over the top of
each queen-cake, ornamenting them, (while the
icing is quite wet) with red and green nonpareils,
or fine sugar-sand, dropped on, carefully, with the
thumb and finger.

When the cakes are iced, set them in a warm
place to dry ; but not too near the fire, as that will
cause the icing to crack.

———◆———

POUND CAKE.

One pound of flour, sifted.
One pound of white sugar, powdered and sifted.
One pound of fresh butter.
Ten eggs.
Half a glass of wine
Half a glass of brandy   } mixed.
Hylf a glass of rose-water
Twelve drops of essence of lemon.
A table-spoonful of mixed mace and cinnamon.
A nutmeg, powdered.

———

Pound the spice and sift it. There should be
twice as much cinnamon as mace. Mix the cinnamon, mace, and nutmeg together.

Sift the flour into a broad pan, or wooden bowl.
Sift the powdered sugar into a large deep pan, and
cut the butter into it, in small pieces. If the weather is very cold, and the butter hard, set the pan
near the fire for a few minutes ; but if the butter is

too warm, the cake will be heavy. Stir the butter and sugar together, with a wooden stick, till they are very light, and white, and look like cream.

Beat the eggs in a broad shallow pan with a wooden egg-beater or whisk. They must be beaten till they are thick and smooth, and of the consistence of boiled custard.

Pour the liquor and rose-water, gradually, into the butter and sugar, stirring all the time. Add, by degrees, the essence of lemon and spice.

Stir the egg and flour alternately into the butter and sugar, a handful of flour, and about two spoonfuls of the egg (which you must continue to beat all the time,) and when all is in, stir the whole mixture very hard, for near ten minutes.

Butter a large tin pan, or a cake-mould, with an open tube rising from the middle. Put the mixture into it as evenly as possible. Bake it in a moderate oven, for two, three, or four hours, in proportion to its thickness, and to the heat of the fire.

When you think it is nearly done, thrust a twig or wooden skewer into it, down to the bottom. If the stick comes out clean and dry, the cake is almost baked. When quite done, it will shrink from the sides of the pan, and cease making a noise. Then withdraw the coals (if baked in a dutch oven) take off the lid, and let the cake remain in the oven to cool gradually.

You may ice it, either warm or cold.

5

BLACK CAKE, OR PLUM CAKE.

One pound of flour, sifted.
One pound of fresh butter.
One pound of powdered white sugar.
Twelve eggs.
Two pounds of the best raisins.
Two pounds of currants.
Two table-spoonfuls of mixed spice, mace and cinnamon.
Two nutmegs, powdered.
A large glass of wine ⎫
A large glass of brandy ⎬ mixed together.
Half a glass of rose-water ⎭
A pound of citron.

———

Pick the currants very clean, and wash them, draining them through a cullender. Wipe them in a towel. Spread them out on a large dish, and set them near the fire or in the hot sun to dry, placing the dish in a slanting position. Having stoned the raisins, cut them in half, and when all are done, sprinkle them well with sifted flour, to prevent their sinking to the bottom of the cake. When the currants are dry, sprinkle them also with flour.

Pound the spice, allowing twice as much cinnamon as mace. Sift it, and mix the mace, nutmeg, and cinnamon together. Mix also the liquor and rose-water, in a tumbler or cup. Cut the citron in slips. Sift the flour into a broad dish. Sift the sugar into a deep earthen pan, and cut the butter into it. Warm it near the fire, if the weather is too cold for it to mix easily. Stir the butter and sugar to a cream.

Beat the eggs as light as possible. Stir them into the butter and sugar alternately with the flour. Stir very hard. Add, gradually, the spice and liquor. Stir the raisins and currants alternately into the mixture, taking care that they are well floured. Stir the whole as hard as possible, for ten minutes after all the ingredients are in.

Cover the bottom and sides of a large tin or earthen pan, with sheets of white paper well buttered, and put into it some of the mixture. Then spread on it some of the citron, which must not be cut too small. Next put a layer of the mixture, and then a layer of citron, and so on till it is all in, having a layer of the mixture at the top.

This cake is always best baked in a baker's oven, and will require four or five hours in proportion to its thickness.

Ice it, next day.

SPUNGE CAKE.

Twelve eggs.
Ten ounces of sifted flour, dried near the fire.
A pound of loaf-sugar, powdered and sifted.
Twelve drops of essence of lemon.
A grated nutmeg.
A tea-spoonful of powdered cinnamon and mace, mixed.

Beat the eggs as light as possible. Eggs for spunge or almond-cakes require more beating than for any other purpose. Beat the sugar, by degrees, into the eggs. Beat very hard, and continue to beat some time after the sugar is all in.

No sort of sugar but loaf, will make light spungecake. Stir in, gradually, the spice and essence of lemon. Then, by degrees put in the flour, a little at a time, stirring round the mixture very slowly with a knife. If the flour is stirred in too hard, the cake will be tough. It must be done lightly and gently, so that the top of the mixture will be covered with bubbles. As soon as the flour is all in, begin to bake it, as setting will injure it.

Put it in small tins, well buttered, or in one large tin pan. The thinner the pans, the better for spunge-cake. Fill the small tins about half full. Grate loaf-sugar over the top of each, before you set them in the oven.

Spunge-cake requires a very quick oven, particularly at the bottom. It should be baked as fast as possible, or it will be tough and heavy, however light it may have been before it went into the oven. It is of all cakes the most liable to be spoiled in baking. When taken out of the tins, the cakes should be spread on a sieve to cool. If baked in one large cake, it should be iced.

A large cake of twelve eggs, should be baked at least an hour in a quick oven.

For small cakes, ten minutes is generally sufficient. If they get very much out of shape in baking, it is a sign that the oven is too slow.

———

Some think that spunge-cakes and almond cakes are lighter, when the yolks and whites of the eggs are beaten in separate pans, and mixed gently together before the sugar is beaten into them.

If done separately from the yolks, the whites should be beaten till they stand alone.

———

ALMOND CAKE.

Two ounces of blanched bitter almonds, pounded very fine.
Seven ounces of flour, sifted and dried.
Ten eggs.
One pound of loaf-sugar, powdered and sifted.
Two table-spoonfuls of rose-water.

———

Take two ounces of shelled bitter almonds, or peach-kernels. Scald them in hot water, and as you peel them, throw them into a bowl of cold water. Then wipe them dry, and pound them one by one in a mortar, till they are quite fine and smooth.

Break ten eggs, putting the yolks in one pan and the whites in another. Beat them separately as light as possible, the whites first, and then the yolks.

Add the sugar, gradually, to the yolks, beating it in very hard. Then, by degrees, beat in the almonds, and then add the rose-water.

Stir half the whites of eggs, into the yolks and sugar. Divide the flour into two equal parts, and stir in one half, slowly and lightly, till it bubbles on the top. Then the other half of the white of egg, and then the remainder of the flour, very lightly.

Butter a large square tin pan, or one made of paste-board, which will be better. Put in the mixture, and set immediately in a quick oven, which must be rather hotter at the bottom than at the top. Bake it according to the thickness. If you allow the oven to get slack, the cake will be spoiled.

Make an icing with the whites of three eggs, twenty-four tea-spoonfuls of loaf-sugar, and eight drops of essence of lemon.

When the cake is cool, mark it in small squares with a knife. Cover it with icing, and ornament it while wet, with nonpareils dropped on in borders, round each square of the cake. When the icing is dry, cut the cake in squares, cutting through the icing very carefully with a penknife. Or you may cut it in squares first, and then ice and ornament each square separately.

5*

FRENCH ALMOND CAKE.

Six ounces of shelled sweet almonds.
Three ounces of shelled bitter almonds, or peach kernels.
Three ounces of sifted flour, dried near the fire.
Fourteen eggs.
One pound of powdered loaf-sugar.
Twelve drops of essence of lemon.

———

Blanch the almonds, by scalding them in hot water. Put them in a bowl of cold water, and wipe them dry, when you take them out. Pound them, one at a time, in a mortar, till they are perfectly smooth. Mix the sweet and bitter almonds together. Prepare them, if possible, the day before the cake is made.

Put the whites and yolks of the eggs, into separate pans. Beat the whites till they stand alone, and then the yolks till they are very thick.

Put the sugar, gradually, to the yolks, beating it in very hard. Add, by degrees, the almonds, still beating very hard. Then put in the essence of lemon. Next, beat in, gradually, the whites of the eggs, continuing to beat for some time after they are all in. Lastly, stir in the flour, as slowly and lightly, as possible.

Butter a large tin mould or pan. Put the cake in, and bake it in a very quick oven, an hour or more, according to its thickness.

The oven must on no account be hotter at the top, than at the bottom.

When done, set it on a sieve to cool.

Ice it, and ornament it with nonpareils.

These almond cakes are generally baked in a turban-shaped mould, and the nonpareils put on, in spots or sprigs.

A pound of almonds in the shells (if the shells are soft and thin,) will generally yield half a pound when shelled. Hard, thick-shelled almonds, seldom yield much more than a quarter of a pound, and should therefore never be bought for cakes or puddings.

Bitter almonds and peach-kernels can always be purchased with the shells off.

———

Families should always save their peach-kernels, as they can be used in cakes, puddings and custards.

———

MACCAROONS.

Half a pound of shelled sweet almonds.
A quarter of a pound of shelled bitter almonds.
The whites of three eggs.
Twenty-four large tea-spoonfuls of powdered loaf-sugar.
A tea-spoonful of rose-water.
A large tea-spoonful of mixed spice, nutmeg, mace and cinnamon.

———

Blanch and pound your almonds, beat them very smooth, and mix the sweet and bitter together ; do them, if you can, the day before you make the maccaroons. Pound and sift your spice. Beat the whites of three eggs till they stand alone ; add to them, very gradually, the powdered sugar, a spoonful at a time, beat it in very hard, and put in, by degrees, the rose-water and spice. Then stir in, gradually, the almonds. The mixture must be like a soft dough ; if too thick, it will be heavy ; if too thin, it will run out of shape. If you find your almonds not sufficient, prepare a few more, and stir them in. When it is all well mixed and stirred, put some flour in the palm of your hand, and taking up a lump of the mixture with a knife, roll it on your hand with the flour into a small round ball; have ready an iron or tin pan, buttered, and lay the maccaroons in it, as you make them up. Place them about two inches apart, in case of their spreading. Bake them about eight or ten minutes in a moderate oven; they should be of a pale brownish colour. If too much baked, they will lose their flavour; if too little, they will be heavy. They should rise high in the middle, and crack on the surface. You may, if you choose, put a larger proportion of spice.

APEES.

A pound of flour, sifted.
Half a pound of butter.
A glass of wine, and a tablespoonful of rose-water, mixed.
Half a pound of powdered white sugar.
A nutmeg, grated.
A tea-spoonful of beaten cinnamon and mace.
Three table-spoonfuls of carraway seeds.

Sift the flour into a broad pan, and cut up the butter in it. Add the carraways, sugar, and spice, and pour in the liquor by degrees, mixing it well with a knife. If the liquor is not sufficient to wet it thoroughly, add enough of cold water to make it a stiff dough. Spread some flour on your pasteboard, take out the dough, and knead it very well with your hands. Put it into small pieces, and knead each separately, then put them all together, and knead the whole in one lump. Roll it out in a sheet about a quarter of an inch thick. Cut it out in round cakes, with the edge of a tumbler, or a tin of that size. Butter an iron pan, and lay the cakes

in it, not too close together. Bake them a few
minutes in a moderate oven, till they are very
slightly coloured, but not brown. If too much baked, they will entirely lose their flavour. Do not
roll them out too thin.

JUMBLES.

Three eggs.
Half a pound of flour, sifted.
Half a pound of butter.
Half a pound of powdered loaf-sugar.
A table-spoonful of rose-water.
A nutmeg grated.
A tea-spoonful of mixed mace and cinnamon.

Stir the sugar and butter to a cream. Beat the
eggs very light. Throw them, all at once, into the
pan of flour. Put in, at once, the butter and sugar, and then add the spice and rose-water. If you
have no rose-water, substitute six or seven drops of
strong essence of lemon, or more, if the essence is
weak. Stir the whole very hard, with a knife.

Spread some flour on your paste-board, and flour
your hands well. Take up with your knife, a portion of the dough, and lay it on the board. Roll it
lightly with your hands, into long thin rolls, which
must be cut into equal lengths, curled up into rings,
and laid gently into an iron or tin pan, buttered,
not too close to each other, as they spread in baking. Bake them in a quick oven about five minutes, and grate loaf-sugar over them when cool.

KISSES.

One pound of the best loaf sugar, powdered and sifted.
The whites of four eggs.
Twelve drops of essence of lemon.
A tea-cup of currant jelly.

———

Beat the whites of four eggs till they stand alone.
Then beat in, gradually, the sugar, a tea-spoonful
at a time. Add the escence of lemon, and beat
the whole very hard.

Lay a wet sheet of paper on the bottom of a
square tin pan. Drop on it, at equal distances, a
small tea-spoonful of stiff currant jelly. With a
large spoon, pile some of the beaten white of egg
and sugar, on each lump of jelly, so as to cover it
entirely. Drop on the mixture as evenly as possible, so as to make the kisses of a round smooth
shape.

Set them in a cool oven, and as soon as they are
coloured, they are done. Then take them out, and
place them two bottoms together. Lay them lightly on a sieve, and dry them in a cool oven, till the
two bottoms stick fast together, so as to form one
ball or oval.

———

SPANISH BUNS.

Four eggs.
Three quarters of a pound of flour, sifted.
Half a pound of powdered white sugar.
Two wine-glasses and a half of rich milk.
Five ounces of fresh butter.
A wine-glass and a half of the best yeast.
A table-spoonful of rose-water.
A grated nutmeg.
A large tea-spoonful of powdered mace and cinnamon.

———

Sift half a pound of flour into a broad pan, and
sift a quarter of a pound, separately, into a deep

plate, and set it aside. Put the milk into a soup-plate, cut up the butter, and set it on the stove or near the fire to warm, but do not let it get too hot. When the butter is very soft, stir it all through the milk with a knife, and set it away to cool. Beat the eggs very light and mix the milk and butter with them, all at once; then pour all into the pan of flour. Put in the spice, and the rose-water, or if you prefer it, eight drops of essence of lemon; Add the yeast, of which an increased quantity will be necessary, if it is not very strong and fresh. Stir the whole very hard, with a knife. Add the sugar gradually. If the sugar is not stirred in slowly, a little at a time, the buns will be heavy. Then, by degrees, sprinkle in the remaining quarter of a pound of flour. Stir all well together; butter a square iron pan, and put in the mixture. Cover it with a cloth, and set it near the fire to rise. It will probably not be light in less than five hours. When it is risen very high, and is covered with bubbles, bake it in a moderate oven, about a quarter of an hour or more, in proportion to its thickness.

When it is quite cool, cut it in squares, and grate loaf-sugar over them. This quantity will make twelve or fifteen buns.

They are best the day they are baked.

___

You may, if you choose, bake them separately, in small square tins, adding to the batter half a pound of currants or chopped raisins, well floured, and stirred in at the last.

___

In making buns, stir the yeast well before you put it in, having first poured off the beer or thin part from the top. If your yeast is not good, do not attempt to make buns with it, as they will never be light.

Buns may be made in a plainer way, with the following ingredients, mixed in the above manner.

———

Half a pound of flour, sifted into a pan.
A quarter of a pound of flour, sifted inaplate, and set aside to sprinkle in at the last.
Three eggs, well beaten.
A quarter of a pound of powdered sugar.
Three wine-glasses of milk.
A wine-glass and a half of the best yeast.
A large tea-spoonful of powdered cinnamon.
A quarter of a pound of butter, cut up, and warmed in the milk.

———

RUSK.

A quarter of a pound of powdered sugar.
A quarter of a pound of fresh butter.
One pound of flour sifted.
One egg.
Three wine-glasses of milk.
A wine-glass and a half of the best yeast.
A table-spoonful of rose-water.
A tea-spoonful of powdered cinnamon.

Sift your flour into a pan. Cut up the butter in the milk, and warm them a little, so as to soften the butter, but not to melt it entirely. Beat your egg ; pour the milk and butter into your pan of flour, then the egg, then the rose-water and spice, and lastly the yeast. Stir all well together with a knife.

Spread some flour on your paste-board : lay the dough on it, and knead it well. Then divide it into small pieces of an equal size, and knead each piece into a little thick round cake. Butter an iron pan, lay the cakes in it, and set them in a warm place to rise. Prick the tops with a fork. When they are quite light, bake them in a moderate oven.

INDIAN POUND CAKE.

Eight eggs.
The weight of eight eggs in powdered sugar.
The weight of six eggs in Indian meal, sifted.
Half a pound of butter.
One nutmeg, grated,—or a tea-spoonful of cinnamon.

———

Stir the butter and sugar to a cream. Beat the eggs very light. Stir the meal and eggs, alternately, into the butter and sugar. Grate in the nutmeg. Stir all well. Butter a tin pan, put in the mixture, and bake it in a moderate oven.

———

CUP CAKE.

Five eggs.
Two large tea-cups full of molasses.
The same of brown sugar, rolled fine.
The same of fresh butter.
One cup of rich milk.
Five cups of flour, sifted.
Half a cup of powdered allspice and cloves.
Half a cup of ginger.

———

Cut up the butter in the milk, and warm them slightly. Warm also the molasses, and stir it into the milk and butter: then stir in, gradually, the sugar, and set it away to get cool.

Beat the eggs very light, and stir them into the mixture alternately with the flour. Add the ginger and other spice, and stir the whole very hard.

Butter small tins, nearly fill them with the mixture, and bake the cakes in a moderate oven.

6

LOAF CAKE.

Two pounds of sifted flour, setting aside half a pound to sprinkle in at the last.
One pound of fresh butter.
One pound of powdered sugar.
Four eggs.
One pound of raisins, stoned, and cut in half.
One pound of, currants, washed and dried.
Half a pint of milk.
A glass of wine.
A glass of brandy.
A table-spoonful of mixed spice, mace, nutmeg and cinnamon.
Half a pint of the best brewer's yeast; or more, if the yeast is not very strong.

———

Cut up the butter in the milk, and warm it till the butter is quite soft ; then stir it together, and set it away to cool. It must not be made too warm. After you have beaten the eggs, mix them with the butter and milk, and stir the whole into the pan of flour. Add the spice and liquor, and stir in the sugar gradually. Having poured off the thin part from the top, stir the yeast, and pour it into the mixture. Then sprinkle in the remainder of the flour.

Have ready the fruit, which must be well floured, stir it gradually into the mixture. Butter a large tin pan, and put the cake into it. Cover it, and set it in a warm place for five or six hours to rise. When quite light, bake it in a moderate oven.

———

SUGAR BISCUITS.

Three pounds of flour, sifted.
One pound of butter.
A pound and a half of powdered sugar.
Half a pint of milk.
Two table-spoonfuls of brandy.
A small tea-spoonful of pearl-ash dissolved in water.
Four table-spoonfuls of carraway seeds.

———

Cut the butter into the flour. Add the sugar and carraway seeds. Pour in the brandy, and then the milk. Lastly, put in the pearl-ash. Stir all well with a knife, and mix it thoroughly, till it becomes a lump of dough.

Flour your paste-board, and lay the dough on it. Knead it very well. Divide it into eight or ten pieces, and knead each piece separately. Then put them all together, and knead them very well in one lump.

Cut the dough in half, and roll it out into sheets, about half an inch thick. Beat the sheets of dough very hard, on both sides, with the rolling-pin. Cut them out into round cakes with the edge of a tumbler. Butter iron pans, and lay the cakes in them. Bake them of a very pale brown. If done too much they will lose their taste.

These cakes kept in a stone jar, closely covered from the air, will continue perfectly good for several months.

MILK BISCUITS.

Two pounds of flour, sifted.
Half a pound of butter.
Two eggs.
Six wine-glasses of milk.
Two wine-glasses of the best brewer's yeast, or three of good home-made yeast.

Cut the butter into the milk, and warm it slightly on the top of the stove, or near the fire. Sift the flour into a pan, and pour the milk and butter into it. Beat the eggs and pour them in also. Lastly, the yeast. Mix all well together with a knife.

Flour your paste-board, put the lump of dough on it, and knead it very hard. Then cut the dough in small pieces, and knead them into round balls. Stick the tops of them with a fork.

Lay them in buttered pans and set them to rise. They will probably be light in an hour. When they are quite light, put them in a moderate oven and bake them.

———

They are best when quite fresh.

———◆———

BUTTER BISCUITS.

Half a pound of butter.
Two pounds of flour, sifted.
Half a pint of milk, or cold water.
A salt-spoonful of salt.

———

Cut up the butter in the flour, and put the salt to it. Wet it to a stiff dough with the milk or water. Mix it well with a knife.

Throw some flour on the paste-board, take the dough out of the pan, and knead it very well.

Roll it out into a large thick sheet, and beat it very hard on both sides with the rolling-pin. Beat it a long time.

Cut it out with a tin, or cup, into small round thick cakes. Beat each cake on both sides, with the rolling-pin. Prick them with a fork. Put them in buttered pans, and bake them of a light brown in a slow oven.

GINGERBREAD NUTS.

Two pounds of flour, sifted.
One pound of fresh butter.
Half a pound of brown sugar.
One quart of sugar-house molasses.
Two ounces of ginger, or more, if it is not very strong.
Twelve dozen grains of allspice, ⎫
Six dozen cloves, ⎬ powdered and sifted.
Half an ounce of cinnamon, ⎭

———

Cut up the butter in the flour. Spread the sugar on your paste-board, and crush it very fine with the rolling-pin. Put it to the flour and butter, and then add the ginger and other spice. Wet the whole with the molasses, and stir all well together with a knife.

Throw some flour on your paste-board, take the dough (a large handful at a time) and knead it in separate cakes. Then put all together, and knead it very hard for a long time, in one large lump. Cut the lump in half, roll it out in two even sheets, about half an inch thick, and cut it out in little cakes, with a very small tin, about the size of a cent. Lay them in buttered pans, and bake them in a moderate oven, taking care they do not scorch, as gingerbread is more liable to burn than any other cake.

You may, if you choose, shape the gingerbread nuts, by putting flour in your hand, taking a very small piece of the dough, and rolling it into a little round ball.

6*

COMMON GINGERBREAD.

A pint of molasses.
Half a pound of brown sugar.
One pound of fresh butter.
Two pounds and a half of flour sifted.
A pint of milk.
A small tea-spoonful of pearl-ash.
A tea-cup full of ginger.

————

Cut the butter into the flour. Crush the sugar
with a rolling-pin, and throw it into the flour and
butter. Add the ginger.

Having dissolved the pearl-ash in the milk, stir
the milk and molasses alternately into the other ingredients. Stir it very hard for a long time, till it
is quite light.

Put some flour on your paste-board, take out
small portions of the dough, and make it with your
hand into long rolls. Then curl up the rolls into
round cakes, or twist two rolls together, or lay them
in straight lengths or sticks side by side, and touching
each other. Put them carefully in buttered pans,
and bake them in a moderate oven, not hot enough
to burn them. If they should get scorched, scrape
off with a knife, or grater, all the burnt parts, before
you put the cakes away.

You can, if you choose, cut out the dough with
tins, in the shape of hearts, circles, ovals, &c. or
you may bake it all in one, and cut it in squares
when cold.

————

If the mixture appears to be too thin, add, gradually, a little more sifted flour.

LAFAYETTE GINGERBREAD.

Five eggs.
Half a pound of brown sugar.
Half a pound of fresh butter.
A pint of sugar-house molasses.
A pound and a half of flour.
Four table-spoonfuls of ginger.
Two large sticks of cinnamon,
Three dozen grains of allspice, } powdered and sifted.
Three dozen of cloves,
The juice and grated peel of two large lemons.

Stir the butter and sugar to a cream. Beat the
eggs very well. Pour the molasses, at once, into
the butter and sugar. Add the ginger and other
spice, and stir all well together.

Put in the egg and flour alternately, stirring all
the time. Stir the whole very hard, and put in the
lemon at the last. When the whole is mixed, stir
it till very light.

Butter an earthen pan, or a thick tin or iron one,
and put the gingerbread in it. Bake it in a moderate oven, an hour or more, according to its thickness. Take care that it does not burn.

Or you may bake it in small cakes, on little tins.

Its lightness will be much improved by a small
tea-spoonful of pearl-ash dissolved in a table-spoonful of milk, and stirred lightly in at the last. Too
much pearl-ash will give it an unpleasant taste.

If you use pearl-ash, you must omit the lemon,
as its taste will be entirely destroyed by the pearl-
ash. You may substitute for the lemon, some raisins and currants, well floured, to prevent their
sinking.

This is the finest of all gingerbread, but should
not be kept long, as in a few days it becomes very
hard and stale.

A DOVER CAKE.

Half a pint of milk.
A small tea-spoonful of pearl-ash.
One pound of sifted flour.
One pound of powdered white sugar.
Half a pound of butter.
Six eggs.
One glass of brandy.
Half a glass of rose-water.
One grated nutmeg.
A tea-spoonful of powdered cinnamon.

———

Dissolve the pearl-ash in the milk. Stir the sugar and butter to a cream, and add to it, gradually,
the spice and liquor. Beat the eggs very light,
and stir them into the butter and sugar, alternately,
with the flour. Add, gradually, the milk, and stir
the whole very hard.

Butter a large tin pan, and put in the mixture.
Bake it two hours or more in a moderate oven. If
not thick, an hour or an hour and a half will be sufficient.

Wrap it in a thick cloth, and keep it from the
air, and it will continue moist and fresh for two
weeks. The pearl-ash will give it a dark colour.

———

It will be much improved by a pound of raisins,
stoned and cut in half, and a pound of currants,
well washed and dried.

Flour the fruit well, and stir it in at the last.

CRULLERS.

Half a pound of butter.
Three quarters of a pound of powdered white sugar.
Six eggs, or seven, if they are small.
Two pounds of flour, sifted.
A grated nutmeg.
A tea-spoonful of powdered cinnamon.
A table-spoonful of rose-water.

Cut the butter into the flour, add the sugar and spice, and mix them well together.

Beat the eggs, and pour them into the pan of flour &c. Add the rose-water, and mix the whole into a dough. If the eggs and rose-water are not found sufficient to wet it, add a very little cold water. Mix the dough very well with a knife.

Spread some flour on your paste-board, take the dough out of the pan, and knead it very well. Cut it into small pieces, and knead each separately. Put all the pieces together, and knead the whole in one lump. Roll it out into a large square sheet, about half an inch thick. Take a jagging-iron, or, if you have not one, a sharp knife ; run it along the sheet, and cut the dough into long narrow slips. Twist them up in various forms. Have ready an iron pan with melted lard. Lay the crullers lightly in it, and fry them of a light brown, turning them with a knife and fork, so as not to break them, and taking care that both sides are equally done.

When sufficiently fried, spread them on a large dish to cool, and grate loaf-sugar over them.

Crullers may be made in a plainer way, with the best brown sugar (rolled very fine,) and without spice or rose-water.

They can be fried, or rather boiled, in a deep
iron pot. They should be done in a large quantity
of lard, and taken out with a skimmer that has holes
in it, and held on the skimmer till the lard drains
from them. If for family use, they can be made
an inch thick.

DOUGH NUTS.

Three pounds of sifted flour.
A pound of powdered sugar.
Three quarters of a pound of butter.
Four eggs.
Half a large tea-cup full of best brewer's yeast.
A pint and a half of milk.
A tea-spoonful of powdered cinnamon.
A grated nutmeg.
A table-spoonful of rose-water.

Cut up the butter in the flour. Add the sugar,
spice, and rose-water. Beat the eggs very light,
and pour them into the mixture. Add the yeast,
(half a tea-cup, or two wine-glasses full,) and then
stir in the milk by degrees, so as to make it a soft
dough. Cover it, and set it to rise.

When quite light, cut it in diamonds with a jagging-iron, or a sharp knife, and fry them in lard.
Grate loaf sugar over them when done.

WAFFLES.

Six eggs.
A pint of milk.
A quarter of a pound of butter.
A quarter of a pound of powdered white sugar.
A pound and a half of flour, sifted.
A tea-spoonful of powdered cinnamon.

Warm the milk slightly. Cut up the butter in it,
and stir it a little. Beat the eggs well, and pour

them into the butter and milk. Sprinkle in half the flour, gradually. Stir in the sugar, by degrees, and add the spice. Stir in, gradually, the remainder of the flour, so that it becomes a thick batter.

Heat your waffle-iron ; then grease it well, and pour in some of the batter. Shut the iron tight, and bake the waffle on both sides, by turning the iron.

As the waffles are baked, spread them out separately on a clean napkin. When enough are done for a plate-full, lay them on a plate in two piles, buttering them, and sprinkling each with beaten cinnamon.

SOFT MUFFINS.

Five eggs.
A quart of milk.
Two ounces of butter.
A large tea-spoonful of salt.
Two large table spoonfuls of brewer's yeast, or four of home-made yeast.
Enough of sifted flour to make a stiff batter.

Warm the milk and butter together, and add to them the salt. Beat the eggs very light, and stir them into the milk and butter. Then stir in the yeast, and lastly, sufficient flour to make a thick batter.

Cover the mixture, and set it to rise, in a warm place, about three hours.

When it is quite light, grease your baking-iron, and your muffin rings. Set the rings on the iron, and pour the batter into them. Bake them a light brown. When you split them to put on the butter, do not cut them with a knife, but pull them open with your hands. Cutting them while hot will make them heavy.

INDIAN BATTER CAKES.

A quart of sifted indian meal, ⎱ mixed.
A handful of wheat flour, sifted, ⎰ mixed.
Three egs, well beaten.
Two table-spoonfuls of fresh brewer's yeast, or four of home-made
  yeast:
A large tea-spoonful of salt.
A quart of milk.

————

Make the milk quite warm, and then put into it
the yeast and salt, stirring them well. Beat the
eggs, and stir them into the mixture. Then, gradually, stir in the flour and indian meal.

Cover the batter, and set it to rise four or five
hours. Or if the weather is cold, and you want
the cakes for breakfast, you may mix the batter late
the night before.

Should you find it sour in the morning, dissolve a
small tea-spoonful of pearl-ash in as much water as
will cover it, and stir it into the batter, letting it sit
afterwards at least half an hour. This will take off
the acid.

Grease your baking-iron, and pour on it a ladle-
full of the batter. When brown on one side, turn
the cake on the other.

————————

FLANNEL CAKES OR CRUMPETS.

Two pounds of flour, sifted.
Four eggs.
Three table-spoonfuls of the best brewer's yeast, or four and a half
  of home-made yeast.
A pint of milk.

————

Mix a tea-spoonful of salt with the flour, and set
the pan before the fire. Then warm the milk,

and stir it into the flour, so as to make a stiff batter. Beat the eggs very light, and stir them into the yeast. Add the eggs and yeast to the batter, and beat all well together: If it is too stiff, add a little more warm milk.

Cover the pan closely, and set it to rise near the fire. Bake it, when quite light.

Have your baking-iron hot. Grease it, and pour on a ladle-full of batter. Let it bake slowly, and when done on one side, turn it on the other.

Butter the cakes, cut them across, and send them to table hot.

ROLLS.

Three pints of flour, sifted.
Two tea-spoonfuls of salt.
Four table-spoonfuls of the best brewer's yeast, or six of home-made yeast.
A pint of luke-warm water.
Half a pint more of warm water, and a little more flour to mix in before the kneading.

Mix the salt with the flour, and make a deep hole in the middle. Stir the warm water into the yeast, and pour it into the hole in the flour. Stir it with a spoon just enough to make a thin batter, and sprinkle some flour over the top. Cover the pan, and set it in a warm place for several hours.

When it is light, add half a pint more of luke-warm water; and make it, with a little more flour, into a dough. Knead it very well for ten minutes.

7

Then divide it into small pieces, and knead each separately. Make them into round cakes or rolls. Cover them, and set them to rise about an hour and a half.

Bake them, and when done, let them remain in the oven, without the lid, for about ten minutes.

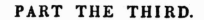

PART THE THIRD.

SWEETMEATS.

GENERAL DIRECTIONS.

In preparing sugar for sweetmeats, let it be entirely dissolved, before you put it on the fire. If you dissolve it in water, allow about half a pint of water to a pound of sugar.

If you boil the sugar before you add the fruit to it, it will be improved in clearness, by passing it through a flannel bag. Skim off the brown scum, all the time it is boiling.

If sweetmeats are boiled too long, they lose their avour, and become of a dark colour.

If boiled too short a time, they will not keep well.

You may ascertain when jelly is done, by dropping a small spoonful into a glass of water.

If it spreads and mixes with the water, it requires more boiling. If it sinks in a lump to the bottom, it is sufficiently done.

Raspberry jelly requires more boiling than any other sort. Black currant jelly less.

7*

APPLE JELLY.

Take the best pippin, or bell-flower apples. No others will make good jelly. Pare, core, and quarter them. Lay them on a brass or bell-metal kettle, and put to them as much water only, as will cover them, and as much lemon-peel as you choose. Boil them till they are soft, but not till they break. Drain off the water through a cullender, and mash the apples with the back of a spoon. Put them into a jelly bag, set a deep dish or pan under it, and squeeze out the juice.

To every pint of juice, allow a pound of loaf-sugar, broken up, and the juice of two lemons. Put the apple-juice, the sugar, and the lemon-juice, into the preserving kettle. Boil it a quarter of an hour, skimming it well. Take it immediately from the kettle, and pour it warm into your glasses, but not so hot as to break them. When cold, cover each glass with white paper dipped in brandy, and tie it down tight with another paper. Keep them in a cool place.

Quince Jelly is made in the same manner, but do not pare them. Quarter them only.

RED CURRANT JELLY.

Wash your currants, drain them, and pick them from the stalks. Mash them with the back of a spoon. Put them in a jelly-bag, and squeeze it till all the juice is pressed out.

To every pint of juice, allow a pound of the best loaf-sugar. Put the juice and the sugar into your kettle, and boil it fiteen minutes, skimming it all the while. Pour it warm into your glasses, set it for several hours in the sun, and when cold, tie it up with brandy paper. Jellies should never be allowed to get cold in the kettle. If boiled too long, they will lose their flavour, and become of a dark colour.

Strawberry, raspberry, blackberry, and grape jelly may be made in the same manner, and with the same proportion of loaf-sugar.

Red currant jelly may also be made in a very simple manner, by putting the currants whole into the kettle, with the sugar ; allowing a pound of sugar to a pound of currants. Boil them together fifteen minutes, skimming carefully. Then pour them into a sieve, with a pan under it. Let them drain through the sieve into the pan, pressing them down with the back of a spoon.

Take the jelly, while warm, out of the pan, and put it into your glasses. Tie it up with brandy paper when cold.

BLACK CURRANT JELLY.

Pick the currants from the stalks, wash and drain them. Mash them soft with a spoon, put them in a bag, and squeeze out the juice. To each pint of juice, allow three quarters of a pound of loaf-sugar. Put the juice and sugar into a preserving kettle, and boil them about ten minutes, skimming them well. Take it immediately out of the kettle. Put it warm into your glasses. Tie it up with brandy papers.

The juice of black currants is so very thick, that it requires less sugar and less boiling than any other jelly.

GOOSEBERRY JELLY.

Cut the gooseberries in half, (they must be green) and put them in a jar closely covered. Set the jar in an oven, or pot filled with boiling water. Keep the water boiling round the jar till the gooseberries are soft, take them out, mash them with a spoon, and put them into a jelly bag to drain. When all the juice is squeezed out, measure it, and to a pint of juice, allow a pound of loaf-sugar. Put the juice and sugar into the preserving kettle, and boil them fifteen minutes, skimming them carefully. Put the jelly warm into your glasses. Tie them up with brandy paper.

Cranberry jelly is made in the same manner.

JELLY OF WILD GRAPES.

Pick the grapes from the stems, wash and drain them. Mash them with a spoon. Put them in the preserving kettle, and cover them closely with a large plate. Boil them ten minutes. Then pour them into your jelly bag, and squeeze out the juice.

Allow a pint of juice to a pound of sugar. Put the sugar and juice into your kettle, and boil them fifteen minutes, skimming them well.

Fill your glasses while the jelly is warm, and tie them up with brandy papers.

———

PEACH JELLY.

Wipe the wool off your peaches, (which should be free-stones, and not too ripe) and cut them in quarters. Crack the stones, and break the kernels small.

Put the peaches and the kernels into a covered jar, set them in boiling water, and let them boil till they are soft.

Strain them through a jelly-bag, till all the juice is squeezed out. Allow a pound of loaf-sugar to a pint of juice. Put the sugar and juice into a preserving kettle, and boil them fifteen minutes, skimming carefully.

Put the jelly warm into your glasses, and when cold, tie them up with brandy paper.

Plum, and green gage jelly may be made in the same manner, with the kernels, which greatly improve the flavour.

———

PRESERVED QUINCES.

Pare and core your quinces, carefully taking out the parts that are knotty and defective. Cut them into quarters, or into round slices. Put them into a preserving kettle, and cover them with the parings and a very little water. Lay a large plate over them to keep in the steam, and boil them till they are tender.

Take out the quinces, and strain the liquor through a bag. To every pint of liquor, allow a pound of loaf-sugar. Boil the juice and sugar together, about ten minutes, skimming it well. Then put in the quinces, and boil them gently twenty minutes. When the sugar seems to have completely penetrated them, take them out, put them in a glass jar, and pour the juice over them warm. Tie them up, when cold, with brandy paper.

———

In preserving fruit that is boiled first without the sugar, it is generally better (after the first boiling) to let it stand till next day before you put the sugar to it.

———

PRESERVED PIPPINS.

Pare and core some of the largest and finest pippins. Put them in your preserving kettle, with some lemon-peel, and all the apple-parings. Add a very little water, and cover them closely. Boil them till they are tender, taking care they do not burn. Take out the apples, and spread them on a large dish to cool. Pour the liquor into a bag, and strain it well. Put it into your kettle with a pound of loaf-sugar to each pint of juice, and add lemon juice to your taste. Boil it five minutes, skimming it well. Then put in the whole apples, and boil them slowly half an hour, or till they are quite soft and clear. Put them, with the juice, into your jars, and when quite cold, tie them up with brandy paper.

Preserved apples are only intended for present use, as they will not keep long.

———

Pears may be done in the same way, either whole or cut in half. They may be flavoured either with lemon or cinnamon, or both. The pears for preserving should be green.

———◆———

PRESERVED PEACHES.

Take the largest and finest free-stone peaches, before they are too ripe. Pare them, and cut them in halves or in quarters. Crack the stones, and take out the kernels, and break them in pieces. Put the peaches, with the parings and kernels, into your preserving kettle, with a very little water. Boil them till they are tender. Take out the peaches and spread them on a large dish to cool. Strain the liquor through a bag or sieve. Next day, measure the juice, and to each pint allow a pound of loaf-sugar. Put the juice and sugar into the kettle with the peaches, and boil them slowly half an hour, or till they are quite soft, skimming all the time. Take the peaches out, put them into your jars, and pour the warm liquor over them. When cold, tie them up with brandy paper.

If boiled too long, they will look dull, and be of a dark colour.

———

If you do not wish the juice to be very thick, do not put it on to boil with the sugar, but first boil the sugar alone, with only as much water as will dissolve it, and skim it well. Let the sugar, in all cases, be entirely melted before it goes on the fire. Having boiled the sugar and water, and skimmed it to a clear syrup, then put in your juice and fruit together, and boil them till completely penetrated with the sugar.

PRESERVED CRAB APPLES.

Wash your fruit. Cover the bottom of your preserving kettle with grape-leaves. Put in the apples. Hang them over the fire, with a very little water, and cover them closely. Do not allow them to boil, but let them simmer gently till they are yellow. Take them out, and spread them on a large dish to cool. Pare and core them. Put them again into the kettle, with fresh vine-leaves under and over them, and a very little water. Hang them over the fire till they are green. Do not let them boil.

Take them out, weigh them, and allow a pound of loaf-sugar to a pound of crab-apples. Put to the sugar just water enough to dissolve it. When it is all melted, put it on the fire, and boil and skim it. Then put in your fruit, and boil the apples till they are quite clear and soft. Put them in jars, and pour the warm liquor over them. When cold, tie them up with brandy paper.

PRESERVED PLUMS.

Cut your plums in half, (they must not be quite ripe,) and take out the stones. Weigh the plums,

and allow a pound of loaf-sugar to a pound of fruit.
Crack the stones, take out the kernels and break
them in pieces. Boil the plums and kernels very
slowly for about fifteen minutes, in as little water as
possible. Then spread them on a large dish to
cool, and strain the liquor.

Next day make your syrup. Melt the sugar in
as little water as will suffice to dissolve it, (about
half a pint of water to a pound of sugar) and boil
it a few minutes, skimming it till quite clear. Then
put in your plums with the liquor, and boil them
fifteen minutes. Put them in jars, pour the juice
over them warm, and tie them up, when cold, with
brandy paper.

———

Syrups may be improved in clearness, by adding
to the dissolved sugar and water, some white of
egg very well beaten, allowing the whites of two
eggs to each pound of sugar. Boil it very hard,
and skim it well, that it may be quite clear before
you put in your fruit.

PRESERVED STRAWBERRIES.

Weigh the strawberries after you have picked off
the stems. To each pound of fruit allow a pound
of loaf-sugar, which must be powdered. Strew
half of the sugar over the strawberries, and let
them stand in a cold place two or three hours.
Then put them in a preserving kettle over a slow
fire, and by degrees strew on the rest of the sugar.
Boil them fifteen or twenty minutes, and skim them
well.

8

Put them in wide-mouthed bottles, and when cold, seal the corks.

If you wish to do them whole, take them carefully out of the syrup, (one at a time) while boiling. Spread them to cool on large dishes, not letting the strawberries touch each other, and when cool, return them to the syrup, and boil them a little longer. Repeat this several times.

Keep the bottles in dry sand, in a place that is cool and not damp.

———

Gooseberries, currants, raspberries, cherries and grapes may be done in the same manner. The stones must be taken from the cherries (which should be morellas, or the largest and best red cherries) and the seeds should be extracted from the grapes with the sharp point of a penknife. Gooseberries, grapes, and cherries, require longer boiling than strawberries, raspberries or currants.

———

PRESERVED CRANBERRIES.

Wash your cranberries, weigh them, and to each pound allow a pound of loaf-sugar. Dissolve the sugar in a very little water, (about half a pint of water to a pound of sugar) and set it on the fire in a preserving kettle. Boil it near ten minutes, skimming it well. Then put in your cranberries, and boil them slowly, till they are quite soft, and of a fine colour.

Put them warm into your jars or glasses, and tie them up with brandy paper, when cold.

———

All sorts of sweetmeats keep better in glasses, than in stone or earthen jars. When opened for use, they should be tied up again immediately, as exposure to the air spoils them.

Common glass tumblers are very convenient for jellies, and preserved small fruit. White jars are better than stone or earthen, for large fruit.

PRESERVED PUMPKINS.

Cut slices from a fine high-coloured pumpkin, and cut the slices into chips about the thickness of a dollar. The chips should be of an equal size, six inches in length, and an inch broad. Weigh them, and allow to each pound of pumpkin chips, a pound of loaf sugar. Have ready a sufficient number of fine lemons, pare off the yellow rind, and lay it aside. Cut the lemons in half, and squeeze the juice into a bowl. Allow a jill of juice to each pound of pumpkin.

Put the pumpkin into a broad pan, laying the sugar among it. Pour the lemon-juice over it. Cover the pan, and let the pumpkin chips, sugar and lemon-juice, set all night.

Early in the morning put the whole into a preserving pan, and boil all together (skimming it well) till the pumpkin becomes clear and crisp, but not till it breaks. It should have the appearance of lemon-candy. You may, if you choose, put some lemon-peel with it, cut in very small pieces.

Half an hour's boiling (or a little more) is generally sufficient.

When it is done, take out the pumpkin, spread it on a large dish, and strain the syrup through a bag. Put the pumpkin into your jars or glasses, pour the syrup over it, and tie it up with brandy paper.

If properly done, this is a very fine sweetmeat. The taste of the pumpkin will be lost in that of the lemon and sugar, and the syrup is particularly pleasant. It is eaten without cream, like preserved ginger. It may be laid on puff-paste shells, after they are baked.

PRESERVED PINE-APPLE.

Pare your pine-apples, and cut them in thin round slices. Weigh the slices, and to each pound allow a pound of loaf-sugar. Dissolve the sugar in a very small quantity of water, stir it, and set it over the fire in a preserving-kettle. Boil it ten minutes, skimming it well. Then put in it the pine-apple slices, and boil them till they are clear and soft, but not till they break. About half an hour (or perhaps less time) will suffice. Let them cool in a large dish or pan, before you put them into your jars, which you must do carefully, lest they break. Pour the syrup over them. Tie them up with brandy-paper.

RASPBERRY JAM.

Allow a pound of sugar to a pound of fruit. Mash the raspberries, and put them with the sugar into your preserving kettle. Boil it slowly for an hour, skimming it well. Tie it up with brandy paper.

All jams are made in the same manner.

FINIS.